My First Trip

My First Trip to the Library

Greg Roza

illustrated by
Aurora Aguilera

PowerKiDS press.

New York

Published in 2020 by The Rosen Publishing Group, Inc.
29 East 21st Street, New York, NY 10010

First Edition

Editor: Elizabeth Krajnik
Art Director: Michael Flynn
Book Design: Ricardo Córdoba
Illustrator: Aurora Aguilera

Cataloging-in-Publication Data

Names: Roza, Greg, author.
Title: My first trip to the library / Greg Roza.
Description: New York : PowerKids Press, [2020] | Series: My first trip | Includes index.
Identifiers: LCCN 2018024113| ISBN 9781538344354 (library bound) | ISBN 9781538345641 (pbk.) |
   ISBN 9781538345658 (6 pack)
Subjects: LCSH: Libraries–Juvenile literature. | Librarians–Juvenile literature.
Classification: LCC Z665.5 .R69 2020 | DDC 910.914/6

Manufactured in the United States of America

CPSIA Compliance Information: Batch #CSPK19. For further information contact Rosen Publishing, New York, New York at 1-800-237-9932.

Contents

My name is Jayla.
My Aunt Alexis is a librarian.

Aunt Alexis is taking me to the library.

She works here.

This is my first trip to the library.
It's so big!

The library has ramps for me
to get around easily.

I see some friends from school.

The library has computers.

Aunt Alexis and I play a game!

The library has music.

The library has movies too.

I can do crafts at the library.

My friends and I make
origami animals!

"Where are the books?" I ask Aunt Alexis. "Don't libraries have books?"

"They sure do," Aunt Alexis says.

18

Look at all the books!

Aunt Alexis picks a book
about a turtle named Tilly.

She reads the
book to me. It's
so funny!

Aunt Alexis loves being a librarian.
Maybe someday I will be a librarian.

23

Words to Know

computer

origami

ramp

Index

B
book, 16, 19, 20, 21

C
crafts, 14

L
librarian, 4, 22

T
trip, 7